MM

TO________________________________

SMALL WORLD LIBRARY

JUNIOR WOODCHUCK JAMBOREE

An Adventure in the U.S.A.

GROLIER ENTERPRISES INC.

DANBURY, CONNECTICUT

Developed by The Walt Disney Company in conjunction with Nancy Hall, Inc.
ISBN 0-7172-8214-7

It was the first day of the Junior Woodchuck Jamboree. Woodchucks from all over the United States were busily setting up camp just outside of Washington, D.C., the nation's capital. Uncle Donald was there as a den leader, joining his nephews Huey, Dewey, and Louie.

Each Junior Woodchuck had brought something from home to share with the others. Huey, Dewey, and Louie brought a prize-winning squash from Grandma Duck's farm as part of their exhibit.

HAWAii
Troop 203
Arizona
Troop 17

Huey, Dewey, and Louie had made lots of friends already. Rafael from New Mexico showed them crystals he had found in the caves near his home. Danny from Colorado had brought a dinosaur bone that he had dug up outside his town. And Jane from Florida was showing off some interesting seashells, when all of a sudden something knocked into her table.

"What was that?" asked Huey, as everyone bent down to look underneath the table.

"Why, it's a little animal," said Jane. "I think he wants us to play with him!"

Just as Jane reached out for the little animal, he darted out from beneath the table and led his new friends on a merry chase around the camp.

The animal ran to the California exhibit, where the surfboards made a perfect slide for him. Down he slid, right into the path of some Junior Woodchucks from New York City, who were riding their skateboards.

"That was a close one!" said one of the skateboarders. "Where did he come from?"

"We don't know," said Louie, "but there he goes!"

The Woodchucks followed the animal over to the Mississippi exhibit, where a raft was being built. The playful creature quickly scampered over the raft and headed for one of the Native American exhibits, where he jumped into a canoe.

"Now we've got him!" said Huey. But as Huey climbed into the canoe, the animal jumped into the river and swam across to the other side.

"He certainly did want to play!" said Louie as they watched him disappear behind the trees. "I'm afraid we've lost him now."

"Maybe we'll see him again," said Dewey. "Let's go see the rest of the exhibits."

The next morning the Junior Woodchucks began a day of sightseeing. Their first stop was the National Zoo. They saw elephants, lions, monkeys, and even pandas that had come all the way from China.

They were on their way to see the tigers when Huey stopped in his tracks.

“Do you see that sign?” he said to the others. “It says that an otter has escaped from the zoo! Do you think that the animal we were playing with was an otter?”

“It looked just like that picture,” said Jane. The other Woodchucks agreed.

Dewey pulled out his Junior Woodchuck Guidebook.
"Let's see," he said. "It says here that otters are extremely playful animals who love to swim and slide on their bellies."
"That sounds like the animal we saw," said Danny.
"There's a long list of places where otters can be found in the United States," continued Dewey, "but Washington, D.C., isn't one of them."

“That little guy just has to be the runaway otter!” said Jane. “Wouldn’t it be great if we could find him and bring him back to the zoo safe and sound?”

“Don’t get your hopes up,” said Donald. “It’s difficult to catch an otter. They’re very clever, you know. Besides, you won’t have any time—we have too many sights to see.”

The Woodchucks left the zoo and continued on to the Washington Monument. They rode the elevator all the way to the top of the high tower.

"What a view!" said Rafael.

"You're not kidding!" agreed Louie, handing him the binoculars. "Do you see what I see?"

"Wow!" said Rafael. "It's the otter! He's in the Reflecting Pool!"

The Junior Woodchucks raced down to the Reflecting Pool. When they reached the otter, he playfully swam down to the other end of the pool and hopped out.

"Follow that otter!" shouted Jane.

"Hey, wait a minute!" said Donald. "Our bus is over this way!"

Donald reluctantly joined the chase. The Woodchucks followed the otter down the mall—and right into the Smithsonian Institution!

"Well, the Museum of American History was our next scheduled stop, anyway," said Donald, panting.

"We'd better split up," said Huey. "This museum is very big."

Jane and Louie took off down a corridor.

"Uh-oh," said Jane, standing in front of the First Ladies exhibit. "I think that fur stole is moving!"

A woman next to Jane looked at the mannequin and let out a loud scream. As the guards ran over to help the woman, the otter unwrapped himself from the mannequin and scurried away.

"Come on!" said Louie. But it was too late. The otter had disappeared again.

Donald finally rounded up all the Woodchucks and led them back to the bus. Then they headed off to the Lincoln Memorial.

"Abraham Lincoln was our sixteenth president," said Huey. "I learned that in school."

"That's right, Huey," said Donald. "And President Lincoln believed that everyone should be free."

"Does that include otters?" shouted Louie, pointing at the steps.

They all watched as the otter slid down the wall beside the steps leading away from the monument. They started to follow him, but Donald stopped them.

"Oh, no," Donald said. "We're done chasing otters today. It's time to get back to the campground."

"We can't leave yet!" cried Huey. "We haven't caught the otter."

"Someone else will have to find it," Donald replied firmly. "We've got to get going now."

The Woodchucks were very quiet on the bus ride back to camp. They were thinking about the otter, and all the sights they had seen.

"Did you notice that everywhere we went, the otter was there, too?" asked Dewey.

Huey pulled out his guidebook again to see if he had missed anything.

"Listen to this!" he said. "It says, 'The otter loves to play games. It is not uncommon for it to play follow-the-leader or hide-and-seek with other otters or human beings.' "

"So the whole time we thought we were chasing the otter, he may have been playing games with us!" exclaimed Rafael.

"He'll probably never find us now," said Jane sadly.

Back at the campground, Donald decided to go catch some fish for dinner. The Junior Woodchucks were busily preparing the camp fire when suddenly they heard a loud noise.

"It's coming from Uncle Donald's tent," said Louie.

"What is it?" asked Danny.

"Maybe it's a bear!" said Jane.

"Well, there's only one way to find out," said Huey bravely. He carefully pulled back the tent flaps.

"It's the otter," Huey shouted. "And he's gotten into everything!"

When the little otter saw the Woodchucks, he dropped the jar he was holding and ran off into the woods.

The Woodchucks took off after the otter. They were determined to catch him this time.

The otter led them to the river bank and dived in. He splashed around for a while, and then he swam away. The otter looked back towards the shore, as if he hoped the Woodchucks would find some way to follow him.

Luckily, the rafts and canoes were still by the river. The Woodchucks jumped in and the chase was on.

But the otter quickly grew tired of swimming. To make the chase a little more interesting, he decided to continue his game of follow-the-leader in the woods.

"Let's try roping him," said Willie, a Woodchuck from Texas. He threw the other Woodchucks some ropes. "Grab these!"

The Woodchucks spun the ropes over their heads and let them fly.

"Shucks!" said Willie. "It looks like you all could use a few roping lessons."

Katie, a Woodchuck from Maine, had brought a fish net with her.

"If we surprise the otter with this net, he'll never get away," she said. "We catch lots of fish like this all the time back home."

But the only thing the Woodchucks were able to capture in the big, wide net was each other!

“Uncle Donald was right,” said Huey. “That little rascal is smarter than we are. Where in the world could he be now?”

“Over there!” cried Rafael.

They all stared as the otter rolled playfully on the ground and then scampered away.

“Here we go again!” said Jane, as everyone took off after him.

They discovered the otter sitting quietly next to Donald, snacking on some fish.

"Hey, get out of here!" said Donald to the otter. "Those are my fish!"

"The guidebook says that fish is an otter's favorite food, Uncle Donald," said Huey. "The otter must be hungry."

Donald kindly gave the Woodchucks more fish to feed to the otter. After the tired little animal was finished eating, he fell asleep in Donald's knapsack.

The next morning Donald and the Junior Woodchucks brought the otter back to the zoo. The zookeeper was very happy to have the otter back. And the mother otter was overjoyed to see her pup again.

The zookeeper invited all the Woodchucks to stay and help out at feeding time.

"Do I get to share his dinner now?" asked Donald with a smile as he threw some fish to the otter.

Donald and the Woodchucks boarded the bus to head back to the campground.

"I'm so proud of the way you Woodchucks worked together to help rescue the otter," Donald told them.

"And I'm happy that we all have so many new friends from all over the country," added Louie. "That's what has made this adventure so special."

The other Woodchucks couldn't have agreed more.

Did You Know...?

Fifty states make up the United States of America. The Junior Woodchucks in this story come from different parts of the country. Since the United States is one of the largest countries in the world, both in land and population, there are many exciting things to see and do. Here are some of the interesting things you might find if you traveled around this country:

Washington, D.C., is the capital of the United States and one of the nation's most beautiful cities. Each spring, thousands of cherry trees bloom with lovely flowers all over this city.

The National Air and Space Museum is one of the seven Smithsonian Museums on the Washington Mall. This museum contains air balloons and modern spacecraft, as well as rocks brought back from the moon by astronauts.

The pandas in Washington's National Zoo are a gift from the Chinese government. The zoo contains about 3,000 animals.

The Statue of Liberty, a gift to the United States from France, stands at the entrance to New York Harbor. It is a symbol of the United States and the freedom that this country represents to millions of people all over the world.

Carlsbad Caverns in New Mexico has hundreds of connected underground caves. Millions of bats live in Bat Cave, which is at the entrance to the caverns.

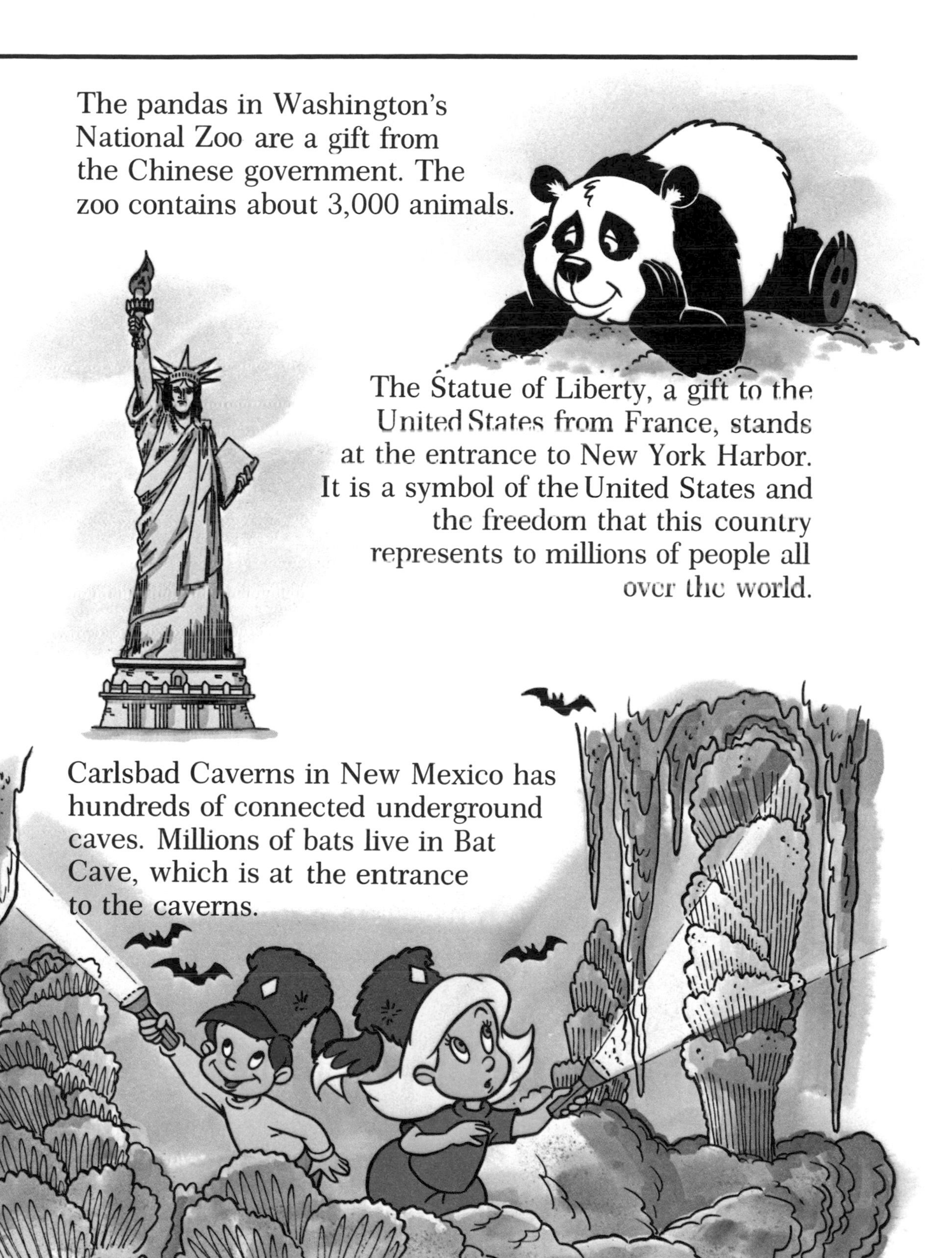

Hawaii is known as the Aloha State because of its friendliness to visitors. *Aloha* (ah-loh-ha) means “love” in Hawaiian. Visitors eat at outdoor feasts called *luaus* (loo-ows) and watch Hawaiians perform the traditional *hula* (hoo-la) dance.

Fishermen in Maine catch more lobsters than fishermen in any other state. The shellfish are caught in traps called “lobster pots.” Maine is also known for its beautiful lakes and forests.

San Francisco is
one of California's most
spectacular cities. Old-fashioned
cable cars climb some of the
city's many steep streets.

Texas is one of the few states where cowboys still herd
cattle. In rodeo contests, cowboys compete against one
another at riding wild horses and roping calves.
Ride 'em, Donald!

OLD FAITHFUL
N
W
E
S